False
Reflections

First paperback edition October 2022

Book cover design by Nirkri@fiverr

ISBN 978-1-7367559-2-1 (paperback)
ISBN 978-1-7367559-3-8 (ebook)

www.trisharrowsmithauthor.com

For all of my supporters

I appreciate each and every one of you.

Writing this sequel has taught me a lot and I'm so grateful you asked me to write it.

Thank you!

Chapter I

"I'm sorry, Max. I can't help you anymore."

Maxwell's face fell for a brief moment before the corners of his mouth turned up. "Glad you're in a joking mood, but I'm not. I don't have much time before someone comes looking for them."

The doctor stared, straight faced, over Maxwell's shoulder. "I can't help you. I thought I had more time to help them." His eyes closed and he shook his head. "I'm sorry."

Maxwell shifted forward to step inside when he heard a boot hit the bottom step of the porch. He paused.

"Maxwell Lewis? You're under arrest for kidnapping and murder. Move slowly and put your hands behind your back."

He stared at his brother. "After everything I've done for you? You betrayed me."

Chapter II

The interrogation room was freezing. Maxwell wished he had changed into more appropriate clothing, but he was planning on digging a hole, not sitting in a cement room. He'd been locked in for over two hours already and not a single person had been in to check on him. He was getting restless. It was already late in the day and he was supposed to be getting married the next afternoon.

He laid his head on the table and was drifting off to sleep when a detective walked in. He stood and reached his hand out to greet him. "Detective."

He looked down at Maxwell's hand and back to his face. "This isn't a social call, Mr. Lewis. Sit down."

Maxwell obeyed but the look on his face told him he wasn't planning on playing along. "Can we get the questions over with? I've been in this room for hours. I'm tired and I'm getting married tomorrow."

The detective glanced at him and reached forward to pull out his own chair. "Mr. Lewis. I don't think you quite understand how much trouble you're in here. Let me see if I can make it clear to you. You are never getting married again. In fact, you're never going to see outside of prison walls again."

Maxwell stared at him with his head cocked to the side. His face didn't show any sign of emotion.

"Before we start, it may be beneficial for you to know that we've just had a rather lengthy conversation with your brother. We also have an entire team of officers going over every inch of your properties. All of your wives and children are currently under our care and supervision. I would highly suggest telling us the truth, with as much detail as you can, if you ever want a chance of seeing daylight again."

He crossed his arms and leaned back in his chair. Sighing, he rolled his eyes. "Sounds like you already know everything. But falling in love with more than one woman isn't a crime."

"In your case, it should be." He leaned over and hit the record button on a small remote. *"Why don't we start way back at the beginning. Tell me about your parents."*

Maxwell was huddled next to his dresser behind the open closet door. His younger brother, Kenneth, was hiding in the corner, crying, covered by a blanket. Any time their parents would fight he sought comfort in his brother's room. Maxwell protected him when no one else would.

At nine years old, Maxwell had learned to stay as far away from his mother as he could when she was mad, especially when she had been drinking. His father only kept her away for so long. He would stand his ground but only until it got to the point that she reached out and hit him. Then, he would get angry and walk out. At times, he would go to the basement and sleep on the couch. Other times, he would get in his car and drive away, no doubt spending hours at a bar and then sleeping it off in a hotel. Either way, the two boys were left to fend for themselves.

Maxwell wasn't very strong physically, but mentally he was much stronger than his brother. He was convinced Kenneth never would have survived this long if it wasn't for his guidance and protection.

From his position in his bedroom, Maxwell listened to the kitchen door slam shut, followed by the sound of his father's car starting. He immediately began dreading the inevitable. The house had become stale and silent as soon as his father drove away. Maxwell could feel his heart pounding in his chest.

"Kenneth." His mother shouted and they could hear her footsteps as she ascended the stairs.

Maxwell jumped up. "You, stay here. Lock the door behind me."

"Max?"

"Stay here." He opened the door open just wide enough to slip out before pulling it shut behind him. He held tight to the knob until he heard the lock click.

"Where's your brother?"

He squared his shoulders and stepped away from the door. "He's safe. Away from you." His voice exuded a confidence he didn't feel. He would protect his brother every chance he got but he wished his father would do the same for him. Instead, Maxwell saw him as a coward. He loved his father, but during times like this he hated him with every ounce of his being.

His mother stepped forward and slapped his face hard enough for his head to turn sideways. The hot, tingling sensation set in immediately. "I brought you into this world, Maxwell..."

"I know, you can take me out of it." He always tried to be strong while not making her any angrier. But, he stood, feeling his heart trying to escape from his chest, and he heard his brother whimper from behind the door. Something in him broke. He couldn't explain the new feeling but all of a sudden he felt courageous, strong, powerful. He didn't see his mother as a monster anymore, he saw her as an enemy that needed to be defeated. He pulled his eyes from the floor and looked straight into hers. "Try it, bitch."

Before he could react, she lunged at him, slamming him into the wall, pinning him by his shoulders. She held her face barely an inch from his. Her breath was hot and thick, it burned his nose anytime he drew a breath in. "I don't know who you think you are, but you will never speak to me like that again. Do you hear me? Never." Spit flew from her mouth and landed on Maxwell's cheek.

"You will not treat me like this again. Ever." He pulled his arms toward his chest and pushed as hard as he could. He watched her, as if in slow motion, stumble backward. One foot caught on the other and her body crumpled and tumbled down the stairs. There was a landing halfway down and once the shock wore off, Maxwell cautiously walked toward the staircase, stopping at the top step, and peered down. He could see that she was breathing but she wasn't moving.

He turned back and banged on his bedroom door with both fists. "Come on. Hurry up. We're leaving." He continued banging until he felt the door give way. His brother's weary face appeared in the crack. "Let's go. We're going to call Grandma." He led his brother down the steps, trying to shield him from the sight of his mother. It didn't work as he had planned and Kenneth let out a piercing scream.

Maxwell paused, slowly turning to look at his mother, hoping the scream hadn't disturbed her. He felt relieved when he saw that she hadn't stirred. He pulled his brother down the rest of the stairs and they ran out the front door.

They ran all the way to a corner store, nearly half a mile away. Maxwell had to slow down numerous times to allow Kenneth to catch up. Once they got to the parking lot, both boys stopped and rested their hands on their knees, struggling to catch their breath.

Once Maxwell recovered enough, he stood straight and dug a dime out of his pocket. He lifted the receiver of the payphone to his ear and struggled to slide the coin into the pay slot. His heart was still pounding and his entire body was shaking and covered in sweat. Once he managed to drop the coin in, he dialed his grandparent's number. To calm his nerves, he counted the number of rings before his grandmother picked up. Seven.

"Grandma? It's me, Maxwell." That was all he managed to get out before the tears spilled onto his cheeks. After five minutes of doing his best to answer all her questions, he hung up the phone and he and Kenneth sat on the curb while they waited for their grandmother to pick them up. Their grandfather would be calling an ambulance and driving over to their house to check on their mother.

Fifteen minutes later, Maxwell recognized the blue Buick that had pulled up. Their grandmother rounded the front of the car and hugged them each in turn before they both piled into the backseat. The trip to their grandparents was silent.

By the time they arrived, there was a police cruiser parked at the corner of the driveway. "Am I in trouble, Grandma?"

"No, Max. Just tell the officers what happened. Answer their questions honestly." She stepped out of the car and waved to the officers. They had remained in the car, watching the movements of the three of them until that point.

They all congregated in the large sitting room; it was Maxwell's least favorite room in the house. It always seemed cold to him. There was a large bookcase on the far wall, dotted with sculptures that didn't look like they took any talent at all. His grandmother had told him he would learn to appreciate them as he aged but he never believed her. He also never had any interest in the books. His grandfather tried once to explain the rarity while also admitting that he had never read any of them. Maxwell thought they must have been boring since they had been written so long ago and he wondered why his grandparents spent so much money on useless things.

Everything in this room was so expensive he was afraid to touch any of it. The Victorian couch and two chairs were velvet and had buttons that pulled the fabric into a diamond shaped pattern. It always made sitting uncomfortable, which furthered his hatred of the room.

The officer with the nametag that read "Shapiro" was the first to speak. "So, Maxwell? Is it okay if I call you Max?"

The frightened child from less than an hour before was gone and an attitude fit for a teenager emerged. "I don't care."

The flat of his grandmother's hand connected with the back of his head. "Manners."

"Sorry, Grandma. Yes, sir, you can call me Max."

"Okay. First, I'd like to tell you that your mom should be just fine. They're going to take her to the hospital to get checked out but it's just a precaution." He waited, trying to gauge the reaction on the boys' faces. Neither seemed to care either way. "Now, do you have idea where your father might be?"

Kenneth shrugged and Maxwell shook his head. "My mom told me once that he goes to a bar and then shacks up with some floozy."

His grandmother's mouth dropped open and she rested her hand on his knee. "Um. Usually, if he spends the night away from home, he rents a hotel room. I'm not sure where. I've told him he's more than welcome to stay here but he never does."

"Can you tell me how often this happens?"

Her face fell and her body stiffened. "At least a few times a month. I keep telling him to leave her. She was bad news from the very beginning. We never cared for her much."

The officers didn't seem to care about how she felt about her. They both turned to stare at Maxwell. "Can you tell us what happened this evening?"

"My mom was drinking alcohol. Her and my dad fight a lot when she drinks."

"Mhm. Is that what happened tonight? Your dad got mad at her?"

"Yeah. But then he left."

"Did you see what happened? Did he push her?"

Maxwell sank into the couch and lowered his eyes to his lap. In a barely audible voice he mumbled, "I did."

The officers looked at each other. "I'm sorry. Could you repeat that, please?"

"I did it. I pushed her. I didn't want her to hurt my brother."

"Why did you think she would hurt him?"

"Because she always does. As soon as my dad leaves, she comes looking for us." Maxwell was struggling to fight back his tears. It was the first time he had ever told anyone other than his grandmother that his mother often hit the two of them.

Shapiro hesitated before asking the next question. "I need to ask you a very important question and I need you to be honest with me. Can you do that?"

Maxwell nodded his head.

"You just told us your mother hurts you after your father leaves. I need to know," he paused to clear his throat. "Are you trying to protect your dad?"

He tilted his head and squinted his eyes, unsure what the officer was asking.

"Now, just a minute, officer." His grandmother's face had grown crimson with anger.

"Ma'am, we just need to ask. Young boys will often try to side with their father, even if he's the one who has done something wrong."

"My grandson is not a liar."

"We're not claiming he is. It's just, in most cases of familial violence, it's a male perpetrator. We're simply trying to make sure the information we receive is accurate."

"Well, I don't like what you're implying."

"My dad never hurt me. I pushed my mom because she pushed me into a wall and I wanted her to let me go. I didn't mean to hurt her. I didn't know what to do so we left and I called my grandma."

"We heard that you went all the way to the gas station to call her. Why didn't you call her from your house?"

"I was scared. I was afraid she would wake up and come after me or my brother."

Kenneth remained silent until that point. He wasn't crying but the officers could see he was trying to hold back his tears.

"Did you see what happened?"

He shook his head but didn't speak.

"Have either of your parents ever hurt you before?"

He nodded this time. "My mom. She was yelling for me tonight. I hid in Maxwell's room until she stopped yelling."

"And what happened after she stopped yelling?"

"Max came and got me. He told me we had to leave. I saw Mommy laying on the stairs. Then we ran and called Grandma."

The officer stood and closed his notebook when his radio alerted him they hadn't had any luck locating the boys' father.

Their grandmother stood to walk the officers out. "No need to ask, the boys can stay with us for the night. If their father can't find them when he gets home, this is the first place he'll look."

The officers nodded and took their leave.

The boys' father waited two days before going to pick them up. Maxwell had all but convinced himself that his parents were never coming back. He had never physically harmed her until that evening and he believed she would never forgive him.

When they arrived at the house, the table was set and dinner was ready just as it always was at that time of day. Their mother started a conversation like she normally would, the only difference in their evening was the large bandage on her head.

Maxwell wanted to apologize to her, tell her he didn't mean it. But part of him wasn't sorry. He did it to protect himself and Kenneth. He stayed silent, half-hoping she would say something. The other half of him wanted to forget the entire incident. Nothing was said about it by either of them all evening.

Even though Maxwell had told her numerous times that he was too old to be tucked in, she followed him into his bedroom that night. After pulling his blankets around him, she leaned forward and kissed his forehead gently. It sent a response of ease through his body until she grabbed the hair on the top of his head. "Don't think for a minute that I'm going to forget this." She reached over and turned off the lamp on his bedside table before closing the door behind her.

Maxwell's body tensed as he stared at the closed door in the darkness. His mother's voice had been so calm, so quiet. It sounded sweet, but Maxwell knew better. For the next three months, he would lie awake in his bed, waiting for her to prove to him that she remembered.

With his door closed, he could scarcely hear his parents' voices in the kitchen below. They were arguing again. He heard a door slam in the distance and he waited, his breath slow, so he could hear any sounds of his mother approaching. He didn't know how long he laid there but he drifted off to sleep. It had been long enough that his mind told him he could safely do so.

In his dreams, he heard his mother's voice coming from down the hall. He heard a door slam and a glass break against the floor. A small whimper cut through the remaining silence, a child. "Max." The scream ripped into his dream and jolted him awake.

He sat upright, his heart pounding. He heard another scream followed by a number of thumps. He practically fell out of his bed and ran to the door. His mother was leaning against the railing at the top of the stairs, staring at him.

Maxwell knew immediately what happened and he rushed down the stairs to his brother's aid. His mother watched and laughed as he reached the bottom. "Don't pretend that you can protect him now. The damage is already done. You weren't there for him when he needed you." She threw her head back and released another hearty laugh before retreating to her bedroom.

He remained huddled on the floor, pulling his brother to him. Cradling him like a father to a young child, while he silently cried.

Chapter III

"Your father never tried to help you?"

Maxwell shook his head. "He was never really an involved participant in our lives. He was home every day but he wasn't the type to go out and play catch or help us with a school project. I think he thought just being there was enough."

"Oh? Were you an active participant in your children's lives?"

He sighed. "That's different. They had siblings around all the time, other kids to play with."

"Mhm. But you had your brother and school mates. Why is it different?"

"Because we could see other boys doing things with their father. We knew we were different. Me children didn't know any better."

The detective remained silent for a moment, trying to figure out how those two situations were different. "So, you think it's something that's learned? Not something they just know they need?"

"Exactly."

"Okay. And when you started taking your older boys with you to ball games and things of that sort, do you think it changed anything about the way they felt?"

"I don't think so. They had no idea what was going on. They stood by my side like I told them to and remained quiet."

"You believe they were completely oblivious to everything happening around them? You really don't think they noticed all the other fathers there, watching their boys play?"

Maxwell laughed, amused by the questions. "Detective? I think you're giving these kids way too much credit. I know you're looking at me and thinking my children have to be highly intelligent and...going by that, I can understand why. But, you've met their mothers. None of them are that smart. I lucked out with Allison. And Cayden, my oldest, I don't know if he takes after me or her but he's the smartest one by far. The rest of them, they take after their mothers. Very unfortunate."

"You had a teacher and a nurse as wives. You didn't think they were smart?"

"Oh, detective. Book smart, maybe. Common sense? They didn't possess a single ounce of that. If you would have met Kathleen, you would have laughed and thought I was trying to play a trick on you. That one was dumb as they come."

He sat there with his eyes closed, pinching the bridge of his nose. How could someone speak so poorly about a woman they claimed to have loved? "Let's go back to your father. He must have known you were being abused?"

"He did. Of course, he did. He just didn't care. He would hide in the basement or leave when things got bad. But he never once tried to stop her. The only person in our house he ever defended was himself. It was easy for him because he had to the option to just drive away. Kenneth and I weren't able to do that."

"Did you love him?"

Maxwell leaned back and thought hard about his answer. "Him? No, I didn't love him. I loved the idea of him."

Maxwell had just celebrated his fifteenth birthday. The only thing he had asked his parents for was a vacation in Maldives. Destination vacations were Maxwell's favorite. It was the only time he ever felt truly comfortable and safe around his parents. If they were on vacation, they didn't need to worry about any harm coming their way. They spent ten days exploring the islands and learning about the local culture. All four of them were upset when they had to leave. Maxwell didn't know it at the time, but that trip would be the last thing he ever asked his parents for.

It was the Friday night following their return home. They had just finished eating dinner and his parents had retreated to their bedroom to get ready to go out. Maxwell and his brother cleaned up the kitchen table and counters like they did every Friday. It was a routine neither of them minded. They had a maid five days a week but her schedule allowed for an early exit on Fridays and weekends and holidays off.

Maxwell had often witnessed his mother giving the maid tips and small gifts she picked up for her while on vacation. Part of him thought he would rather be a maid than one of her children. She always seemed to be treated better than the boys were.

They were almost done filling the dishwasher when their mother called down the stairs. "Maxwell? Make your father and I a drink before we leave." It was another Friday night routine. Since the boys had gotten old enough to stay by themselves, the request was a sign they would be leaving soon. Normally, that meant the boys would be heading out, as well, to hang out with friends. Maxwell hadn't made any plans that night.

The weather stations had been predicting a blizzard that would extend well into the next morning. It had already begun to snow. Maxwell looked at his brother and sighed. "Go pick out a movie. I'll bring us some root beer and popcorn."

Kenneth left and went into their game room. It was a large space designed specifically for them. It contained a puffy couch, a big television, a foosball/air hockey table, a dart board, and a pinball machine. Both boys loved it and so did their friends.

Once Maxwell was sure his brother was out of the room, he pulled four glasses from the cabinet and fished a plastic vial from the front pocket of his jeans. He filled the two large glasses with root beer and dumped whiskey into the two squat glasses. He opened the vial, careful not to spill any of its contents on the counter, and tapped a little bit of white powder into the soda glasses and the remainder was dumped into one of the whiskey glasses.

He poured popcorn into the top of the air popper, set a bowl underneath it, and carried the two of the glasses into the game room before bringing the two whiskey glasses to his parents in the sitting room. He hated admitting it, but his mother looked stunning in her black and gold, sequined dress. She was a beautiful woman and Maxwell had inherited many of her traits. His brother looked more like their father's side of the family.

Maxwell sat with them quietly while they finished their drinks. Neither of them believed in savoring the flavor of the alcohol even though they spent a lot of money to indulge in only the highest quality. He walked them to the door, they said their goodbyes, and he locked the door behind them.

He gathered their whiskey glasses and placed them in the dishwasher before grabbing the bowl of popcorn and joining his brother.

"I thought we could watch Terminator one and two since we're not going anywhere."

"Sounds good to me." He set the bowl between them and tried to relax while he waited for the movie to begin.

He was struggling, reaching for his glass on the table before remembering he couldn't drink it yet. He wished he had thought of getting some water as well. They were only about twenty-five minutes into the movie when Kenneth slumped to his side.

That was the moment Maxwell had been waiting for. He drank his entire glass of soda at once, walked the dishes to the kitchen, dumping out the remaining popcorn, loading them int he dishwasher, and starting the wash cycle. He went back to the game room and tried to wake up his brother to tell him to go upstairs to his room. It proved to be much harder than he thought it would be.

He maneuvered him to a standing position and draped his arm around his shoulders. "Hey. I need you to help me out. We need to get upstairs to our own rooms."

His brother's head fell forward. "I don't feel very well. I'm so tired." His eyes closed; his knees buckled. Maxwell was thankful for the grip he had around his brother's waist. He started to slowly move forward, pulling his brother along. "I know. I'm tired, too. We just have to make it up the stairs and then we can sleep."

Kenneth could do little more than drag his feet. At the base of the staircase, Maxwell turned him and wrapped his arms under his brother's so he could pull him up the stairs backwards. By the time they got to the first landing, Maxwell needed to take a break. His eyelids were beginning to get heavy and he could barely keep them open. His muscles were tiring. He sat on the landing and pulled his brother beside him. Maxwell's head fell forward and he snapped it back up. They couldn't sleep on the stairs...

Just after three in the morning, the front door flew open. Maxwell's grandmother entered the house followed by a number of police officers. "Oh, my God. Maxwell?" Her voice came out as little more than a whisper and she rushed toward the stairs. She kneeled before her grandchildren and touched both their faces, hoping for some sign of life. Both boys were lying on their backs with their legs dangling on the stairs below them. They stirred beneath her touch but neither awoke. She turned to the two officers who were ascending the stairs. "They're alive."

An officer nodded in acknowledgment. "Let's get them some medical attention." A third officer, still standing in the doorway, radioed in for an ambulance.

Maxwell's grandmother had shifted and was holding one hand of each of her grandchildren. "I knew this day would come. She should never have been allowed to have children. My son may be gone but at least she didn't succeed in taking my grandchildren as well." She raised each of the boys' hands in turn and kissed the back of them. "They'll be safe with us now."

The ambulance arrived within ten minutes and their grandmother and the officers made their way down the stairs to allow the emergency crew access to the kids. They took their vitals and loaded each of them onto a stretcher for transport.

Their grandmother made her way to the kitchen and started a pot of coffee. She knew it was going to be a long day.

Three officers followed her in. "Are you not going to meet them at the hospital?"

"I will. As soon as I get some caffeine. I'm not drinking any of what they consider coffee from the cafeteria." She pulled four mugs from the cabinet and filled a small pitcher with milk. "So, what's going to happen to my grandchildren now?"

"Right now, they're being taken to the hospital for a medical assessment. The doctors will most likely run some blood tests to see why they were sleeping on the stairs. And they'll do a full workup to check for any other signs of injury. We will need to question both of them once we get word from the hospital that they're awake. As far as placement for them, you should be able to care for them as a temporary home until we're able to get you all in front of a judge to determine permanent placement. If that's something you want, that is."

"Of course, that's what we want. Those poor boys need some sort of stability in their lives. Lord knows they never had it here with that mother of theirs." Without asking if they wanted any, she filled the four mugs and set them on the table before taking a seat. "I know, I shouldn't speak ill of the dead, but these boys are lucky she hadn't killed them yet."

They spent the next hour discussing the boys' past. Their grandmother explained about all the times the kids had called them and showed up on their doorstep because they needed a safe place to stay. She explained how many times they had called to report the abuse and how the cases were closed almost immediately. "I understand looks can be deceiving. Most people would refuse to believe what was happening in this house because it's so well taken care of. The boys always had the best of everything, they're well mannered. You know what I'm saying? The truth is, though, we cosigned for this house. Their mother's name isn't even on the mortgage. We've been telling people for years that we didn't trust her. If she ever tried to leave my son, she would never get a dime. Everything you see here, the house, the cars, the bank accounts, they all have our name and our son's name. She didn't hold claim to anything. We made sure of that."

The officers continued to write in their spiral notebooks and marked key points they needed to follow-up on. The house and all the finances were first on their list.

The boys were both sitting on the side of the bed, happily chatting away. Their grandmother raced in and kissed both of them on the cheek before the officers asked her to leave the room so they could speak to them alone.

"Excuse me, detective?" The nurse was polite, her brown hair pulled into a short ponytail. "Can I have a minute of your time before you speak to them?"

He nodded and followed her into the hall. She was young and her voice told him she wasn't sure if she should be speaking to him or not. He didn't want her to break confidentiality, but he would be grateful for any information she was willing to give. He remained silent and waited for her to tell him what she wanted.

"I'm not sure how much I should say but there are a few things I think you should know." When he didn't respond, she continued. "We got the preliminary lab reports back and it looks as though both of them had sleeping pills in their system. We didn't want to push too hard, but they both swear they didn't take any. While we were checking them for injuries, the older boy, Maxwell? He has several cracked ribs. When we asked about it, he told us his father hit him with the car. It's unfortunate, but abuse isn't uncommon for us to see. I'm sure you know that. But the weird thing is, Maxwell kept telling us it was his father. Kenneth kept saying it was his mother who was hurting them." She cast her eyes to the floor. "I don't know which one is telling the truth, but I do know someone is hurting those kids."

"Thank you." He nodded his head again in appreciation and walked back into the room. "How are you both feeling?"

"I feel okay but I'm still tired. My head feels heavy."

"The nurse told me you two had sleeping pills in your body. Do you take them often?"

Maxwell shook his head. "We didn't take anything. We ate dinner. After our parents left, we had popcorn and watched a movie."

"Do you have any idea how it would have gotten into your system?"

Both boys were silent but shook their heads. Before speaking with the nurse, the detective secured a small meeting room so they could talk to the children individually.

"Maxwell? Are you up for taking a short walk with me?"

"Uh, sure." He slid off the edge of the bed. "Can we get some food? I'm really hungry."

"I think your grandma said she was going to make you breakfast when you leave here." He ushered him into the small room. With the desk sitting in the middle, it felt no larger than a closet.

Maxwell claimed the large, rolling chair behind the desk, leaving the detective to sit in the creaking, wooden chair opposite. "Oh. My parents aren't coming to pick us up?"

He sighed. While it was part of his job to break the bad news, he was half-hoping one of the other detectives or nurses had let it slip. "We'll talk about that later. Right now, I need you to answer a few questions for me so we can figure out last night." He fished his notebook from his pocket and flipped it open. "You told us you all ate dinner together. Can you walk me through, in detail, what happened between dinner and when you got to the hospital?"

"We eat dinner together every night. When we finished, my parents went upstairs to get ready and my brother and I cleaned up the kitchen. We weren't going out because of the snow so I told him to go pick out a movie while I made us some popcorn. My mom brought us a couple glasses of soda and then they left."

"What movie did you watch?"

"Terminator."

"Mm. Good choice. What happened after the movie started playing?"

"We didn't watch much of it. I started to feel really tired. I looked over and saw Kenneth already sleeping. So, I cleaned up both of our glasses and then tried to get him to his room. We were both so tired. We must have fallen asleep on the stairs."

"Did you feel okay otherwise? You were just tired?"

Maxwell nodded.

"Okay. Let's change course for a minute. I heard you had some other injuries that are somewhat recent. Can you tell me what happened? Um, specifically with your ribs."

He looked at his lap. It was clear he was uncomfortable talking about it. "I got hit by a car. Not hard. My father was driving. He didn't mean to."

"And what about all your other injuries? You both seem to have a number of healed fractures and broken bones. That's a lot of hospital trips."

"I told you, he didn't mean to hit me. I'd like to see my brother and go home, please."

He sighed and shook his head. "Okay. We can go back. But I have one more question for you before we do. How long has your mother been abusing you?"

The brothers were released into their grandparents' custody after learning of their parents' demise. The detectives promised to be in contact as soon as they had any additional information relating to the fatal car accident.

The detectives compared notes from the interviews of the two boys. Almost everything from the timelines added up except two points. According to his brother, his mother had always been the abusive and he claimed Maxwell was the one who brought them their drinks. Maxwell told them his mother brought the soda and his father was the abuser.

The results from the autopsies came back a week later. The accident report came back at the same time. The snow covered most of the evidence they would have hoped to find about what led to the accident. The initial report suggested it was a typical, weather-related incident. The car slid off the road, down the embankment, and landed head-first in a ball of fire.

The results from the toxicology report made their initial findings of a simple, albeit tragic accident, much more difficult. Like the boys, their father showed a large amount of sleeping pills in his system. Their mother's didn't show any.

Chapter IV

"So, that's when they started questioning you as a suspect. Why, if you were able to plan out this whole, elaborate scheme, did you lie about who was abusing you? If you had just told the truth, they never would have considered you a potential suspect."

"Do you have any idea how I felt, as a fifteen-year-old male, having a woman abuse me? I tried telling people the day I pushed her down the stairs. My grandmother tried telling people. No one would believe that a mother could do that to her children."

"I don't understand. If you were trying to convince people your father was abusing you, why didn't you poison your mother as well, try to make it look like your father did it?"

"You clearly don't understand. I didn't want to admit who it was. But I wanted them to figure it out. What I didn't want was for my brother to betray me. He was supposed to tell them what I said. They weren't supposed to question me as a suspect. That was his fault."

"That's why you wanted to teach him a lesson? Teach him a lesson while he proved his loyalty to you?"

Maxwell nodded.

In less than one month's time, the boys' grandparents were granted full custody. They put their childhood home on the market and it sold immediately. The furnishings were all sent to auction and the profits for both were divided equally and put into trusts for Maxwell and Kenneth. The money would be available to each of them when they turned eighteen.

The family lawyer was brought in to clear Maxwell's name for the accident. Charges were filed against him but after four months, the charges were suddenly dropped with no explanation as to why. He had spent exactly one night in a detention facility and was released back into his grandparents' care.

Maxwell never outright admitted to anyone what he had done. His grandfather largely ignored him, speaking to him only when absolutely necessary. His grandmother blamed him. She wasted no time letting him know that she knew what he had done, without question. She told him multiple times she understood why he did it but wished he would have left his father out of it.

He understood where she was coming from but what she didn't seem to understand was that his father was just as bad. He knew exactly what was happening and he never once tried to stop it. Maxwell blamed him for a lot of what happened because if he didn't leave every time his parents argued, he could have prevented the worst of it. Maxwell viewed his father as just as much of a monster as he did his mother.

The lawyer that helped Maxwell retired immediately after the charges were dropped and his son took his place. He was happy to take over and be assigned the Lewis estate, but he was wholly unaware of what he was getting himself into.

When Maxwell was seventeen, he decided he might be able to get into his grandfather's good graces by trying to show his respect for the things his grandfather loved. One day over summer break, while his grandparents were out for a day trip, Maxwell took it upon himself to inspect the book collection that resided in the sitting room. The same collection his grandmother told him he would learn to appreciate.

He pulled out the first book and gently flipped through its thin, delicate pages. The smell of the book was overpowering. He returned it to the shelf and pulled out the second. His hope was to find something that would catch his eye. In the fourth book, he found it. It wasn't what he was expecting and it wouldn't bring him any closer to his grandfather, but it was enough to get him everything he wanted in his life. And he knew how the charges against him got dropped so suddenly.

After the death of his parents, Maxwell was never sure he could fully trust his brother. They attended the funeral but neither of them spoke of their mother or father with each other after that day. It was easier for both of them to remain silent. Their relationship with each other hadn't changed much. They spent most of their time together and Maxwell treated Kenneth more like a son than he did a brother.

When Maxwell turned eighteen, he decided to put his brother's loyalty to the test. He wanted to know for sure if he could trust him to stay by his side. He'd already broken that trust once and Maxwell wanted to see if it would happen again.

Kenneth had gotten his learner's permit so Maxwell offered to take him out for a driving lesson. They spent about an hour testing his parking skills. Maxwell set up some cones in an empty parking lot and showed him how to pull into a spot and back into one. It was necessary but he grew bored quickly and he was growing anxious about his plans for when they finished.

"I think that's enough for today."

His brother parked the car one last time and got out to collect the cones. He climbed into the passenger seat. "Thanks for taking me out."

"No problem. Let's go for a drive." It hadn't snowed for a few days, but the roads were still wet from the snow melting during the day and the temperature dropped quickly once the sun went down. They had gone a few miles without saying a word to each other. It was a Sunday evening, and the roads were all but deserted. It happened a lot in the winter. As soon as it started getting dark, everyone went home.

"Where are we going?"

Maxwell put more pressure on the gas pedal. "Just taking a short drive. I thought it'd be fun to see where mom and dad died."

He sank as far into his seat as he could go. "I don't want to do that."

"Sure, you do. It's the perfect time, too, with the anniversary coming up in just a few days." He pressed on the gas pedal again and he could see Kenneth tensing up out of the corner of his eye. Maxwell's lip twitched and he had to fight back the urge to smile. "I've been there a few times. You probably won't be able to see it now because of all the snow but, if you go any other time, there's a big, round patch on the ground that's darker than the rest. It's almost like the remnants of a bonfire, except, you know, it was from their car. Little pieces of burnt wood and debris. It's very therapeutic." He pushed harder on the gas.

"I don't want to see it, Max. I want to go home." Kenneth pleaded with his brother. He had spent the past three years trying to block the images he had made up in his head. Seeing where it happened would make it real for him. He didn't want to know where it happened or see the possible course of events. After the funeral, he put all his efforts into trying to move past it. "Please. Just bring me home. And slow down. You're scaring me."

Maxwell threw his head back and laughed. "I'm scaring you? Do you not trust me? After everything I've done for you?" He had raised his voice and started going faster again. "I don't know if you're aware of this or not but if anything happens to Grandma and Grandpa, I'm going to be your legal guardian. You better trust me, because if you don't, I promise you, I will make your life a living hell."

A sharp curve was coming up on the road ahead. "I trust you. I swear I do. Please, slow down?" Branches that had fractured from the weight of the snow hung low. They reached into the road and scraped across the passenger windows. "Max, please?"

He rolled his eyes and sighed. "Fine." He slammed on the brakes, not realizing the snow had iced over on the shaded edge of the road. The rear of the car kicked out and Maxwell tightened his grip on the steering wheel, trying to correct their direction. He felt Kenneth's head slam into his shoulder. The car spun twice before coming to an abrupt stop when it collided with an ice-covered snowbank.

Maxwell didn't know how much time had passed. He opened his eyes, his vision blurry. It took him some time to remember where he was. The windshield was cracked into multiple spiderwebs. Through them, he could see smoke rising from the hood. He heard a small grumble and looked over to see his brother slumped in the seat.

Leaning over, he tried to push the passenger door open, but it wouldn't budge. He used his shoulder to shove his door open and dragged Kenneth across the driver's seat and pulled him about twenty feet from the car before giving up. He didn't realize how heavy he was and he struggled with his own footing in the snow.

Maxwell had no idea what to do. They were on a main road, but it wasn't highly traveled. He sat in the snow next to Kenneth for a few moments before deciding he had no choice but to walk to get help. His brother stirred as he stood up to leave. All at once it hit him. He couldn't be responsible for causing this accident. After the trouble with his parents, there was no way he would be able to get out of it this time. The police would surely blame him for this one and he would most likely be accused of attempted murder.

He sat back down next to his brother. "Hey. Are you okay?"

Kenneth barely managed to open his eyes and was only able to manage an unintelligible grunt.

"I need you to listen to me. When the cops come, I need you to tell them you were driving."

He struggled to pull himself up to his elbows. "What? You almost just killed me and you want me to lie for you?" He reached up and touched his fingertips to the side of his head. He gasped and the sharp intake of the cold air made him cough.

"It was an accident. I thought you said you trusted me?"

"I do, but..."

"Then tell them it was you. After all that happened with mom and dad, I'll be arrested and you'll be by yourself forever. Grandma and Grandpa aren't leaving you any money. How do you think you're going to survive without me?" He could see headlights coming around the curve where he had lost control of his own car. "Make up your mind now. Do you really think you'll be able to make it without me?"

The car slowed and pulled over to the side of the road. The driver stepped out of his vehicle but stayed behind the open door. "You boys okay?"

Maxwell began to sweat despite the cold temperature. "It was icy." That was all he could manage to get out as his nerves started to take over.

The driver approached them. "Do you need medical attention?"

Kenneth finally spoke up. "No. We're fine, I think. I was going a little too fast."

"If you're sure. There's a gas station a little ways up. I'll call a tow truck for you." In the dark, he couldn't see the patch of blood that Kenneth had left on the snow behind him. "Is there anyone else I can call?"

The boys nodded in unison.

Chapter V

The detective looked bored. "I'm afraid I don't fully understand." He leaned back in his chair and crossed his feet at the ankles. "All you wanted was for your brother to prove to you that he trusted you?"

Maxwell rolled his eyes. "I knew he trusted me. He had to. Without me, our mother would have killed him for sure." He took a sip of water and leaned back in his own chair, mimicking the detective. "Our grandparents were the only family we had. Once they were gone, we were only going to have each other. I wanted proof that he would be there for me, just like I was always there for him."

"I see. And almost killing him and making him take the blame for it was your plan to make that happen?"

He grunted and rubbed at his temples. "The accident was an accident. Yes, it was beneficial to me, but I didn't plan it. We were lucky it wasn't much worse than it was."

"Okay. So, the accident wasn't on purpose. Just dumb luck, I suppose." He flipped the page in his notepad. Even with the recorder running, he preferred to take his own notes. "What was the point of bringing your brother to the place of your parent's accident?"

Maxwell sighed. "I'd been to that spot dozens of times since my parents died. I always felt a sense of peace when I was there. A calm that had never existed before. Freedom."

"You wanted him to feel the same?"

He laughed. "No. I wanted him to prove that I could trust him."

"Did he?"

"Thanks to the accident, yes."

"What if the accident didn't happen? How would he have proved his trust?"

"I was going to admit to him what I had done. If he went back and told my grandparents, I would know I couldn't trust him. But, I thought if he could see how calm I felt in that spot, maybe he would understand why I had to do it. He might realize that I did it for us."

"I'm glad you found you had someone on your side. Tell me about your grandparents.

Something about your relationship with them changed around that time, didn't it?"

A sinister smile crept across Maxwell's face. His body relaxed. He melted into his chair like he was settling in for the evening. "Things definitely changed."

The boys spent three hours in the hospital, waiting for the clearance to go home. Maxwell had a few cuts and bruises, but Kenneth ended up with a few broken ribs, a sprained wrist, and a gash on his head large enough to require eight stitches.

As soon as they got home, their grandmother slammed the front door behind them. "You. Upstairs." She pointed to the split staircase in their entryway. "Maxwell. Don't move until I get back." She followed Kenneth up the stairs to his bedroom and waited while he went in the bathroom to change. She pulled the sheets back and waited for him to climb in like she used to when he was little. "Is the medicine helping your head?"

He nodded and winced. "Yes. As long as I don't move too fast."

"Tell me the truth. Who was driving tonight?"

He closed his eyes. "I was."

She leaned forward and laid a gentle kiss on his forehead. "Get some rest. I'll bring you something to eat in a little while since you didn't get any dinner." She turned his light off and left his door open just enough for a sliver of light to shine through.

Maxwell was still standing in the same spot she had left him. Her heels clacked against the marble floor. She stopped inches from him, raised her hand, and slapped him across the face hard enough for his head to spin to the side. "You're just like your father," she hissed.

His body was tense. He stared at her, his face like stone. A pink welt was beginning to form on his cheek from the chunky ring she wore. "Not exactly. Unfortunately, I got my personality from equal pieces of you and my mother. My father? He's exactly like Grandpa."

"Don't you dare bring your grandfather into this. You could have killed him, Maxwell. I know it was you driving. What were you thinking?"

"Oh. Did he tell you I was driving? Because he told everyone else it was him. Strange that he would change his story now." He turned to leave but his grandmother grabbed his arm, her nails digging into the tender flesh.

"Don't walk away from me. I've protected you your whole life. The least you can do is tell me the truth."

Maxwell yanked his arm free and turned to face her. "Why? So you can deny it like you do everything else?" His eyes were cold. I saw grandpa's pictures. I saw the bank statements. I was supposed to be able to trust you."

"Oh, Max." She reached up and laid her hand gently on his face.

He pulled back. "No, Grandma. Both women in my life, the two I was supposed to trust, the two who were supposed to protect me and Kenneth, and show us undeniable love. You both let us down. Between the abuse and the lies, I'm not going to do it anymore. I'm done pretending we have a happy, loving family."

"What are you going to do?"

"Whatever I have to, to make sure I never have to rely on anyone else again."

Two days later his grandfather called him into the sitting room. He had a glass of whiskey in his hand and an angry look on his face.

Maxwell walked into the room and sat down without speaking.

"Your grandmother told me you upset her the other day." His back was turned toward Maxwell. The ice cubes clinked in his glass as he took a sip.

"Wasn't my intention. I was just being honest with her. She asked me to tell her the truth."

"Sometimes in life, it's best not to say anything. She's your grandmother. She took you in, helped raise you. She deserves your respect. You need to apologize." He turned and looked straight at him.

One side of Maxwell's mouth curled up and he shook his head. "Not a chance."

"I wasn't asking."

"I don't care if you were." He leaned back and propped his feet on the table. The look on his face dared his grandfather to push the issue. He wasn't planning on having this conversation so soon, but the opportunity had presented itself.

His grandfather set his glass on the end table and slapped the bottom of Maxwell's shoe. "Get your feet off my table. What has gotten into you?"

He planted his feet firmly on the floor and sat up, squaring his shoulders. "I'm so glad you asked. A few months ago, I thought it would be a good idea to try to find some common ground, you know, something we could talk about." He paused, waiting for any sign his grandfather knew what he was talking about. Finding none, he continued. "I thought, since you spend so much time in here, the books would have been a great place to start. Do you care to guess what I found?"

He smiled. "I have an idea. I'm guessing that means you want in?"

Maxwell gasped. "Is that a joke? No, I don't want in. What I want, Grandpa, is...financial compensation. All of it. Or...I can expose you for everything you've done and you and Grandma can spend your remaining years in jail."

He picked up his glass and sat in a chair opposite Maxwell. "The firm is already yours, Maxwell. It was supposed to go to your father but," he shrugged. "As soon as you graduate from law school, it'll be yours."

"About law school. I'm not going."

His grandfather almost dropped his glass, whiskey sloshed over the edge. "Excuse me?"

Maxwell almost laughed. He had never heard his grandfather's voice so loud. "I'm not going." Why should I have to work so hard, doing something I have no interest in doing, when I can get it all for free?"

His grandfather had a smug look on his face. "What makes you think you're going to get everything for free? We have well-established lawyers that work for us. Any one of them would be capable of taking over for me. If it goes to one of them, you're out...completely. Plus, you still have your brother. As of now, he stands to get half of everything. More, if he goes to law school and you don't." He stared at his grandson, almost hoping he would argue.

He raised his eyebrows and crossed his arms. "I suppose you have a point. I do still have my brother to worry about." His voice was calm and even. "Except, there are a few problems with that. You and I both know he doesn't have what it takes to be a lawyer. Who's going to hire someone who is afraid of his own shadow? He doesn't have a manipulative bone in his body. And, let's face it, Kenneth really isn't that smart. Do you actually believe he would be able to pass the bar?"

"You've got me there. But you still need to go to school to inherit the business."

"See, that's where you're wrong. You're probably sitting over there, completely carefree, thinking you just need to find a new hiding spot for all the evidence I found against you. You don't. You can leave it all right where it is. I made copies of it all. Every letter, photograph, non-disclosure agreement, bank statements. I have them all."

His grandfather pursed his lips. "What do you want?"

"Everything." Maxwell had no idea if his plan would work but he had to try. He hadn't had a chance to put all the pieces of the puzzle together yet. "I want the money, the house, the business, and guardianship of Kenneth if something happens to you and Grandma before he turns eighteen."

Neither of them said a word for nearly five minutes. "Okay, Maxwell. I'll tell you what. You seem to talk a good game but let's see how serious you are about this." He stood and made a lap around his desk. "We'll make it fun for you. Let's say...We'll give you thirty days to find a woman, make her fall in love with you, and marry you. If you can pull that off, you'll get it all. If not, you give me every piece of evidence you have and Kenneth gets everything."

Before Maxwell could think about what he was getting into, he agreed. "Deal."

His grandfather smirked, believing there would be no way he could figure out how to make that happen.

Maxwell spent his entire evening in his bedroom, trying to come up with a plan. He had no idea how he was going to pull this off. He hadn't even dated a girl exclusively and he was supposed to find one to marry?

He laid in his bed and stared at the ceiling for what felt like hours. Just as he was beginning to drift off, he jolted awake and sat straight up. He knew what he could do.

Chapter VI

If he didn't already know the truth, he never would have believed what he was hearing. "So, tell me, what exactly was your grandfather hiding."

"My grandfather was a betting man. He enjoyed taking risks. But, he also always had a backup plan. Even if he lost, he would never really lose.

"Can you elaborate on what that means?"

"He owned a law firm, but his name wasn't on the business. And of course, back then it was easier to hide who owned it because there wasn't any internet. He had one partner, Ronald Becker, hence the name Becker and Sons, but he only owned twenty percent of the business. He was forced to sign a non-disclosure agreement being offered his share."

"They opened the firm together and he only got twenty percent?"

"Clearly, his partner wasn't a very good businessman. But he did get his name on the building so I guess that much worked out."

"Mhm. And how do you know he was forced to sign the agreement?" The detective was taking detailed notes because this was one area he hadn't been able to confirm yet."

Maxwell laughed. "Because no one would be stupid enough to willingly sign that. Especially a lawyer who knows how to read the fine print." He paused long enough for the detective to finish writing. "Anyway, he had a number of agreements like that. He also had photos of extremely high-powered individuals. Policemen, government officials, judges in, let's say...questionable positions. A lot of photos with scantily clad teenagers. A few girls I went to school with. Plus, the bank statements that showed multiple deposits coming in and nothing going out."

"Where were those deposits coming from?"

"I can't say for sure. But I have a few guesses. He may have been hiding money from the IRS or he was bribing people with the photographs. It is also possible he was offering a buy in for these types of parties. Maybe all three." He shrugged his shoulders indicating he didn't really care either way.

"Tell me about the bet. Obviously, you won?"

He woke up early the next morning and ate a quick breakfast before showering and heading to the city. His first stop was a department store where he spent twenty minutes and two hundred dollars. Next, he stopped at one of his favorite coffee shops, ordered two large cappuccinos, and made his way back to his car.

Maxwell knew exactly where to find her. During the early morning hours, she sat outside the cafe or across the street near a corner store. He was fortunate and found a parking spot right outside the cafe. He had a perfect view of her.

She sat against the wall, her knees pulled into her chest. Her green cargo pants had a rip in one knee, the pockets were deflated, indicating they were empty, and one pant leg was tucked roughly into her combat boot. Maxwell could see where one crocheted mitten was starting to fray at the top and her stringy, blond hair fell from the wool cap pulled tightly over her head. He couldn't help but notice how she kept her head down no matter how many people walked by.

Unlike his grandfather, he didn't have a backup plan. If she didn't listen to him, he would have to play it by ear and adjust his plan as he went. He grabbed the bag from his passenger seat and got out of his car. He walked over and stopped about three feet in front of her. "Get up.

Go put these on and meet me back out here." He held the bag out in her direction.

She barely moved.

"Hey." He nudged the toe of her boot with his shoe and she glanced up at him. "Go put these on and meet me back out here." He shoved the bag toward her again.

She made a move to stand up but hesitated and leaned back against the wall.

The plan was already falling apart. "Let's go. Before I change my mind."

She reached forward, grabbed the bag, and peered into it. Everything had been wrapped in tissue paper and she used her mittened hands to try to peel the wrapping off.

Maxwell sighed. "Will you please go change?"

The girl pulled the bag to her chest and scurried to her feet. She pulled open the cafe door and walked inside. She felt safe there. It was one of the only places that allowed her to use the bathroom without insisting she make a purchase.

While she was inside, Maxwell went back to his car and took a sip of his coffee to warm up. He grabbed the second cup and took it with him. He was waiting on the sidewalk and almost laughed when she emerged. She had traded her cargo pants for jeans and her boot for a pair of pumps. Her mittens were replaced with leather gloves. Maxwell thought he had thought of everything, but he missed a few pieces. Her wool cap still clung to her head and the over-sized khaki jacket was still hanging off her shoulders.

He took the bag, which she had placed all her old clothes in, and handed her the coffee. He pushed the bag into a nearby trash can and she reached out to try to stop him. "It's okay. We'll replace everything." He looked her up and down for a moment and couldn't help but notice the smudges of dirt around her jawline and on her forehead. "Can we get rid of your jacket?"

She grabbed at the opening in a protective manner.

Maxwell shrugged out of his own coat and held it out to her. "You can use mine for now."

She snatched it out of his hand before he had time to change his mind.

He could see her hesitation but watched as she balanced her cup on the edge of the trash can and slowly removed her own coat and handed it to him. He stuffed it in the trash and handed her back her coffee. "Let's go get you cleaned up."

Maxwell unlocked his car and opened the door before he realized she didn't follow him. She still stood in the exact same place, staring at him. He thought, after she changed her clothes, he would be in the clear and she would just follow along. He didn't think he would have to guide her step by step. "Come on. Get in. At least it's warm in here."

He slid into his seat and started the engine. He stared out the windshield for a solid minute before leaning over and rolling down the passenger window. He couldn't hide his annoyance. "Let's go."

The girl made her way hesitantly toward the car with her head down and her shoulders slumped. She dropped into the seat next to him.

They rode in silence for a few minutes before Maxwell asked, "What's your name?."

"Allison."

He could barely hear her whisper over the sound of the car. "Allison. I'm Maxwell. It's nice to meet you." He could feel her staring at him but he chose to ignore it.

After a few moments of awkward silence, Allison found the courage to speak to him. She had removed her gloves and was holding her hands in front of the heating vents. "Where are you taking me?"

"First, we're going to go get your hair cut...and washed." His lip curled up, the disgust in his voice was obvious. "Then, we're going to get you some additional clothes and after that, we'll grab some lunch."

Allison's heart sped up at the word "lunch." She hadn't had a decent meal in months. "Why?"

Maxwell rolled his eyes before glaring at her. "Would you rather spend another night sleeping outside? It's supposed to snow again tonight." There was no further conversation.

They entered the salon and Maxwell approached the front desk. "I'm Maxwell. I called and scheduled a rush appointment a little while ago. Don't worry about price, just do what you can to...," he gestured toward Allison. "Just fix this." He watched as the receptionist's eyes widened at the sight of Allison.

"Okay. Follow me." As she walked by him, Maxwell reached forward and plucked the hat off her head. He dropped it in a trash can behind the desk and claimed a chair in the waiting area. He leaned back and closed his eyes. This initial task was going to be a lot harder than he realized.

He thumbed through all the magazines that were laid out on the table and wished he had thought to bring one of his own. After thirty minutes, he gave up. He leaned back again and stared at the ceiling for nearly an hour before until Allison appeared before him. The first thing he noticed was that they had rinsed away the smudges on her face. He couldn't be more thankful for that.

"Well, she doesn't talk much but she's all cleaned up. Fresh cut, we gave her a nice highlight."

Maxwell didn't acknowledge the conversation. He handed over his credit card, signed the receipt, and dropped a fifty on the counter for a tip. "Let's go."

Allison's jaw dropped when she saw the bill on the counter and she followed him out the door. Her reluctance was starting to ease up.

A bubbly saleswoman greeted them almost as soon as they entered the store. "Welcome. How may I assist you today?" Her smile stretched the full width of her face.

Allison took a step back so she was half hidden behind Maxwell.

"She needs clothes. Five or six new outfits, a pair of shoes, a jacket, and some undergarments."

"I can certainly assist with that, sir. Did you have a budget in mind today?"

Maxwell shook his head. "Just get her what she needs." He walked away without saying anything more.

He made his way to the jewelry counter and picked out a few bracelets, a couple necklaces, and a watch. He didn't get anything terribly expensive but he wanted her to have a few accessories, something to dress her up a bit more.

When he arrived back in the women's department, he saw a folded stack of clothes on the counter and the saleswoman rounded the corner as he approached.

"Oh, good. You're back. I know you said five or six but we found some mix and match pieces so she really has, mmm, maybe nine or ten outfits total."

"That's perfect."

"Oh. I almost forgot. We found a jacket for her like you asked but she also saw a scarf and matching hat that she really liked so I added those as well. I hope you don't mind but I can take them off if you'd like."

"If she actually showed interest in something, it's fine." Just as he finished his sentence, he saw Allison poke her head around a display wall. He laughed; he couldn't help it. She had a playful smile on her face and for the first time that day, he saw a glimmer in her eyes. "Cute hat."

She smiled wider and reached up to touch the puffed edges of the beret. It fit her very well. Her hair fell in blond spirals around her face and her cheeks were glowing pink. She went to stand beside him.

"I just need your credit card and ID, sir."

Maxwell lowered his brows, wondering why she needed his ID.

"It's just that you look so young. It's for security purposes." She still had that wide smile plastered across her face.

He grunted but handed her what she asked for.

Her smile faded as her eyes widened. "Oh. You're a Lewis. I'm so sorry, sir. I didn't know." She handed his license back to him and completed the transaction using as few words as she could. She was clearly embarrassed.

Maxwell drove to a small diner he frequented. He never stayed to eat; usually he ordered and took the food to go. He had no doubt Allison was starving at that point in the day. He had eaten breakfast and his stomach was beginning to rumble.

They sat at the only available table which was located in the middle of the seating area. When the server came over, Maxwell ordered a sandwich and a salad for both of them without asking Allison what she wanted.

While they were waiting for their food to arrive, he tried to engage her in conversation but she would only reply with one or two word answers. She was getting antsy and he wasn't sure if it was all the questions he was throwing at her or if it was the anticipation of getting real food.

As soon as their order arrived, Allison picked up her fork and took one bite after the next without finishing chewing the previous one. Maxwell looked at her and sighed. He reached forward and gently laid his hand on her wrist before she was able to take another bite. She looked over at him, her eyes full of innocence, a leafy green from the salad hanging from the corner of her mouth.

"Could you...slow down a bit and at least pretend you were taught some manners?" He watched her face fall and he instantly regretted his words. He was trying to pull her in, not push her away. "I'm sorry. I didn't mean it the way it sounded. Just...take your time so you don't make yourself sick. All of this food is yours. No one is going to take it from you."

Allison set her fork down and picked up her sandwich. She took one bite and chewed it thoroughly before going for a second.

"Much better."

They walked into the small, one room cabin. Maxwell knew it wasn't much but at least she would have a bed to sleep in and she would be warm. It smelled like burnt wood, stale, but oddly refreshing. "You can stay here tonight. There's a bed and warm blankets. You can take a hot shower but the water runs out quick. There's a television you can watch. I don't have cable, just basic channels."

He went to his car to retrieve the shopping bags and set them inside the door. He held up the small bag of jewelry. "This is yours, too. I'm going to go get you some food for tonight and tomorrow. Is there anything in particular that you need?"

She shook her head. She'd been standing in the same spot since they arrived.

Maxwell thought she might be more comfortable once he left. He built a small fire in the fireplace. "It should warm up in just a few minutes. I'll be back in a little while. Make yourself at home."

He picked up some easy snacks and stuff for sandwiches. He added some basic necessities: a hairbrush, toothbrush, deodorant. He grabbed a romance novel and crossword book from the checkout line so she would have something to do. He dropped everything off at the cabin, showed her how to safely add logs to the fire, and then left her to herself.

The cabin stood by itself on the edge of a small lake. It was secluded and only able to be found if one was specifically looking for it. Across the lake, there was an abandoned beach that afforded a perfect view of the cabin. The last time he was on this stretch of road was the day of the accident with his brother.

The beach area was down a small embankment, the exact one his parent's car had tumbled down. He parked his car a short distance down the road and used his own makeshift path to the beach. Thankful the day had warmed up, he stayed and watched the cabin until the sun began to set. He was surprised Allison never once stepped foot outside the cabin.

He waited until noon the next day to go back to check on her. When he entered the cabin, he found her lounging on the couch with her feet propped on the table, dangerously close to a cereal bowl half-full of milk. She looked over and smiled at him. It was obvious she had slept well and taken advantage of the shower.

She raised her arm so he could see the watch on her wrist. "Thank you." Her voice was soft.

Maxwell smiled. "You're talking today?"

Allison looked at him blankly and shrugged.

"Okay. Is there a reason you're wearing the same clothes as yesterday?"

"They aren't dirty yet." She had turned away from him and began fidgeting with the book in her lap.

He sighed and sat in the torn, upholstered chair. He had to take a minute to remind himself how she was used to living. Even if she wanted to, she didn't have the opportunity to change clothes every day. "Hmm. From now on, let's stick with the rule that you put on a different outfit everyday. Is that okay?" He felt like he was talking to a child but even though he was disgusted by wearing clothes more than once, he wanted to make it clear that she had choices now.

"Okay." She agreed without looking back at him.

"Great. Why don't you go and get changed and we'll grab some lunch."

When she came out of the bathroom, Maxwell gasped. She had put on another pair of jeans, a low-cut boot, a cream, turtleneck sweater, and adorned it with a long, gold chain and mother of pearl pendant. It was only the second day but for the first time, he saw her as a woman instead of a payoff. She was beautiful.

Chapter VII

The detective sat with his head resting in his hand. If he didn't know how the story ended, he would have found it fascinating. Instead, he was doing his best to put the pieces together and focus on the facts. "How did you find the cabin she was staying in?"

Maxwell stood and stretched his back and legs. "Can we take a break?" *We've been talking for hours."*

"Not yet. We've still got quite a bit to cover." *He watched Maxwell slide back into his chair.* "The cabin. How did you find it?"

He rolled his eyes. "I didn't find it. I own it."

The detective raised his eyebrows. "You own it? You were only eighteen."

"That's correct. As soon as I turned eighteen I had access to the account for my *parents' life insurance and from the sale of their house. I used to visit the site on a regular basis. I knew the cabin was there. Once I had access to the money, I waited for the owner to make his monthly visit and I made him an offer he couldn't refuse."*

"So, you could see the cabin from the accident site. I'm guessing that means you can also see the site from the cabin?"

"Correct again. The cabin became my happy place, the spot I could go to to reminisce and celebrate that milestone in my life. I could remember the day I was finally safe."

The detective had to take a few deep breaths. The thought of someone celebrating such a tragic event made his stomach turn. Maxwell had already admitted to killing his parents but the idea that he wanted to relive it time and time again, the knowledge that their demise brought him peace; that was too much for the detective to try to comprehend. "Let's go back to the bet. The first two days you were with her, you just kept throwing money at her. Was that all you had to do to win her over?"

Maxwell laughed heartily. "Oh, no, detective. Money gives you power. It gives you means and opportunity. But it can't make someone fall in love. For that, one needs to possess charm, sophistication...it requires a certain elegance. I just happen to have all of the above."

He was having a difficult time imagining Maxwell possessing any of those traits. "Tell me, then. How did you do it?"

The third day he waited until late afternoon to go check on her. He was impressed that she had a different outfit on and it looked as though she had done some cleaning up. He decided to take her out for an early dinner.

They parked two blocks away. The walk wasn't bad since the day had warmed nicely. Maxwell was explaining to Allison that he wanted her to order for herself since she still didn't seem to want to talk. He was midway through a sentence when he realized she was no longer walking beside him. "Damn." His heart sped up for a moment, thinking she had left.

The city was busy with people leaving work for the day. Fortunately, Allison was tall and her hat was easy to spot among the grey and black suits swarming the sidewalk. He found her staring in the window of a bookstore. "Did you read the book I brought you?"

She nodded without turning her attention to him.

"Let's go get dinner and we'll come back here after we eat."

Reluctantly, she pulled herself away from the store.

They had just finished their appetizers when Allison set her fork down and looked at him. "What does 'You're a Lewis' mean?"

Maxwell was shocked. This was the first time she had started a conversation. He also had no idea what she was talking about. "What?"

"The saleswoman at the store, when you gave her your credit card. She said 'Oh, you're a Lewis.' What does that mean?"

"Oh." Maxwell's shoulders sagged. He used to feel a sense of pride when people would say that. He felt powerful and appreciated, acknowledged. Now, knowing the truth, it made him feel shame and question how much that person really knew. "My grandfather is well-known. He's a lawyer and supports a large number of charities."

"You're rich?"

He couldn't help but laugh. He had to catch himself before he blurted out, "I'm about to be." Instead, he gave her the current truth. "Me? No. But my grandparents have enough money to be more than comfortable."

"Hmm."

As promised, they stopped at the bookstore after dinner. Allison browsed the shelves and picked up one book and put it back when she found one she liked better. Maxwell went behind her and grabbed the ones she put back on the shelf. "You can get more than one. You went through the first one pretty fast."

She had the most grateful look in her eyes and she handed him the last book she pulled out. "Thank you."

Every day for the next two weeks, Maxwell took her out for at least one meal. They spent some time together during the day and she was beginning to open up to him.

Maxwell arrived home around eight one night to find his grandmother waiting for him in the kitchen. As always, she was immaculately dressed.

"Maxwell, let me get you a cup of tea. I'd like to speak with you."

He didn't move. "I don't think we have anything to talk about."

"I think we do." She set a steaming cup of tea in front of an empty chair. "Please, sit down."

Maxwell did as requested. He had no desire to have any sort of conversation with her and the look on his face showed it.

"Your brother misses you. Although, I'm not sure why."

He grunted. "Probably because I'm his brother and I didn't do anything wrong. He could have killed me, you know?" He stared at her with nothing but hate in his eyes. "Anyway. I'm home every day. It's not my fault he's locked away in his room."

"It is your fault. You really hurt him, Maxwell, physically and mentally. And don't try to argue with me. I don't know why he's covering for you but I know he is. He's been locked in his room for weeks and we have to bribe him to even join us for dinner. You need to talk to him. At least convince him to go to school."

"No, I don't need to talk to him. And as far as school goes, that's your job. Last I checked, you're his guardian, not me."

Her face was drawn and she wrapped her hands around her tea cup. "That's the other thing I wanted to talk to you about." She looked at him with sorrow in her eyes. "Your grandfather told me about your bet. Did you really think this through? You graduated from high school early, you have a full scholarship to one of the best schools in the country, and you're not going to go?"

"I don't have to. I can do none of the work and get everything I want anyway."

"And the marriage? Is that where you've been the past few weeks? Trying to convince some poor girl to marry you so you can get what you want?"

He nodded. He was also cringing from the sound of her gold and onyx ring tapping against the side of her cup. It was a clear sign that she was beginning to get agitated.

"Did he tell you he did the same thing with your father? Well, opposite circumstances but the same offer."

Maxwell took a sip of his tea and his lip curled up. Bitter. And he hated tea. "No."

"He did. Except, in your father's case, he was trying to convince him not to marry your mother. He offered him everything if he would walk away from the relationship."

Maxwell laughed until tears stung his eyes. "Grandpa offered him everything and he still married that bitch?" He paused a moment to reflect on what she had just told him. "Why didn't he listen and take the money?"

"Rebellion, I guess. He was young. He wanted to do everything his own way."

"Mhm. Look where that got him."

She sighed. "It didn't get him anywhere. You're the one at fault for where he ended up. But that's not what I want to talk about. You don't think you're doing the exact same thing?"

"No. I can walk away whenever I want. Even if we got divorced and she took half of everything, I'd still have more than enough to live comfortably for my entire life."

This time she couldn't help but laugh. "If you know that and you're already planning for the worst case scenario, why don't you just call it off and share everything fifty-fifty with Kenneth?"

He raised his eyebrows and pursed his lips, unsure of whether to be honest with her or not. The truth was, he already knew Allison was never going to leave him. A prenuptial agreement would take care of that. If she left, she wouldn't get a dime of his money. He decided not to share that information with her. "Where's the fun in that?"

"That's what this is all about? You're only doing it for your own entertainment?"

"I guess I take after grandpa more than either of us realized." He stared at her with his lip curled on one side. "But, no. That's not the main reason. It's just an added bonus. I'm not doing it for the entertainment, I'm doing it based on principal. You know as well as I do, Kenneth has no rightful claim to any of this."

His grandmother almost dropped her teacup. Her mouth fell open. "I...I don't know what you mean."

He watched her hand shake as she tried to place her cup on the saucer. "You know exactly what I mean. Grandpa kept all the paperwork neatly stored in one place. There's a non-disclosure agreement, a bank statement showing a huge deposit, and the forms legally signing over the parental rights. Kenneth has no blood relation to your side of the family which makes me the sole heir to everything. Shall I show you the evidence?"

A single tear ran down her cheek. "I'm so sorry we didn't tell you."

Kenneth banged on Maxwell's door early the next morning and let himself in. "Why are you doing this to us? Do you not care about me at all?"

"I'm doing this for us. I'm making sure none of his money goes anywhere except to us. What do you think is going to happen if something happens to them before you turn eighteen? You won't have access to anything, you'll have to live with strangers. You really do need to think about the future."

"I don't want to think about grandma and grandpa dying. They're all we have left."

"We'll still have each other. That's why I'm doing this." He was making up the words as he went alone, hoping his brother believed him. He was confident in his plan, just like he was the one with Allison. This was his way of ensuring Kenneth could never walk away.

"Can't we just keep it that way? Why do you have to bring someone else in?"

"You'll feel the need, too, when you're older. But for now, this is the way it has to be." It was this way because he wasn't letting the money or his brother go. He guided Kenneth out of his room. "If you really want to know the full story about why I'm doing this, you should talk to grandma."

He spent the next week getting to know everything he could about Allison. Now that she was talking, he asked her every question he could think of about her family, her childhood, her life living on the streets. At first, he was only looking for information that he would be able to use to his advantage. After getting to know more about her, he began to realize he was asking questions because he genuinely cared about the answer.

He spent two days in a mental spiral, arguing with himself about what he was doing. He wasn't supposed to care about her. And he certainly wasn't supposed to find himself falling in love with her.

He took her to an expensive restaurant for dinner and had planned on telling her how he felt. For the first time, she had decided to ask him about his family and the idea of being honest with her melted away. He couldn't tell her the truth about his family. He was no longer proud of his name, his family, or anything they stood for. Like he had with Kenneth a few days before, he made up the answers as he went along and hoped he could remember them if and when the time came.

As he had done every day prior, he walked her into the cabin when they got back. Allison turned to look at him and stood mere inches from his face. Without taking the time to think about what he was doing, he slid his arms around her waist and pulled her close.

They spent the night wrapped in each other's arms. Maxwell woke only a few minutes before her. He stayed in the same position and gently kissed her forehead when she stirred. "Good morning."

"Morning." She gave him the most genuine smile he had seen yet.

He went out to make a pot of coffee while she showered and got dressed. When she joined him in what would be considered the kitchen, he wrapped his arms around her. "I know this is probably sudden but I have to tell you, I have never had feelings like this toward another person. For the past week, every time I leave, all I can think about is when I can come back to see you. And when I am here, I have to force myself to leave. I don't want to do that anymore. Allison, I'm love with you and I want to be with you forever."

She didn't know what to say. Her mouth opened but no words came out.

He could see her chest rising and falling with every breath she took and he knew she liked the idea as much as he did. "Will you marry me?"

She nodded her head and stepped toward him, burying her face in his chest.

Chapter VIII

"So, what happened?"

"We were married four days later. You don't really have to wait for anything when you have money and connections. The day I showed my grandfather my marriage license, he signed everything over to me." Maxwell was growing bored. He understood an hour into the questioning process that he wasn't ever leaving. They had plenty of evidence against him. What he didn't understand was why they needed to ask so many questions and why they wanted so many details. He knew his run was over and so did they.

"And your brother? We didn't hear anything about him only being your half-brother."

"He wouldn't tell you. He was proud of the Lewis name even though he wasn't a true Lewis."

"When did he finally find out?"

"He asked my grandmother like I told him he should. He didn't speak to me for almost six months after that. The next time he talked to me was at my grandfather's funeral. I guess he realized then it really would be just the two of us soon."

"What about your grandmother?"

"Well, she was around for almost a year. She got sick and ended up in the hospital for four days with pneumonia. It eventually took her out."

The detective shook his head. If it wasn't for the way he spoke about Allison, he would believe Maxwell was a full-on psychopath; no remorse, no guilt, no genuine feelings for anyone except Allison. He had that superficial charm that he used to lure women in and then manipulated them to get them to stay. He planned every move he made and his crimes were unknown for years. Allison was the key to understanding Maxwell. "Did Allison ever meet your family?"

Maxwell looked surprised by the question. "A few times. She never spent more than an hour with any of them."

"What happened to Kenneth around that time? He was only seventeen when your grandmother died, correct?"

Three days after his grandmother's passing, Maxwell received the death certificate and was immediately granted custody of Kenneth. He didn't care that it was only four months until he turned eighteen. The first thing he did was force his brother to legally change his name to what it should have been from the beginning. It didn't take much convincing on Maxwell's part since Kenneth was left with nothing. Maxwell had full control over everything he did and he made it clear that if Kenneth wanted anything, he would do as he was told.

Kenneth had never fully grown out of his obedient childhood phase. If an adult told him to do something, he would do so without any hesitation. The only person he ever argued with was Maxwell and even then he would give in. Now that Maxwell had custody and full control over the finances, Kenneth could be easily manipulated to do anything he wanted.

After changing Kenneth's name, Maxwell focused on selling everything his grandparents' owned. He sold their cars, the house, he auctioned the furniture and all of their antique and collectible items, including the books his grandfather loved so dearly.

With the growing sum of money, Maxwell bought Kenneth a small home on the outskirts of the city. It wasn't anything extravagant like they were used to Maxwell had grown to love the simplicity of the lakeside cabin and he believed Kenneth would learn to like the same.

During his teenage years, Maxwell had grown to hate the exchange of gifts for the expectation of love. He longed for the feeling of going home to someone who genuinely cared to see him. His entire life, he was surrounded by toys, movies, video games. But all the stuff began to suffocate him. He felt empty inside. More than anything, he wanted someone to show him they cared. He needed someone to tell him they loved him, they were proud of him, he wanted to feel wanted. Those were the things his family was never able to provide. They could give anything with monetary value, but nothing more.

Maxwell stayed in the cabin with Allison for two years. He had already purchased a large plot of land a few hours from where they currently resided and was in the process of building a second house on it. He came home one evening to find Allison curled in a ball on the couch. "What's the matter?"

She looked at him through teary eyes, her cheeks pink. "I think I might be pregnant."

"Why are you upset about that?" Maxwell snickered even though he tried to control it. He couldn't imagine why this would upset her. They had never discussed the idea of children. They hadn't talked at all about the future. When they married, they were both focused on the present.

Maxwell wanted the money and Allison wanted security. They both benefited from the marriage but neither of them had thought beyond the immediate need. It wasn't until his grandmother died that Maxwell began thinking about what he wanted. Of course, Allison didn't know what he had planned.

She sat up and leaned against his shoulder. "Maxwell. I don't know anything about how to be a mother. I certainly didn't have one that was any good at it and I barely kept myself alive while I was on my own. How am I supposed to care for a child?"

Maxwell draped his arm around her shoulder. "But you did stay alive. You did what you had to do to make that happen. And you'll do the same thing with a child. Everything will come naturally to you."

Allison started to cry again. "I don't think I can do this."

"You don't have to. We'll do this...together."

Maxwell consoled her as much as he was able but it didn't seem that anything he said made her feel better. He understood her confusion and knew why she was scared. He didn't know the first thing about raising a child either. But he was willing to learn. What he wasn't willing to do was raise a child in a town where everyone knew who he was. He had done his best to keep Allison a secret from as many people as he was able and he would do the same with his child. He didn't want

Allison to know how he was raised or what kind of lifestyle he was used to. He fully planned on keeping as much of his past in the past as he could.

He left Allison to deal with her own emotions and set out for Kenneth's house. He wasn't quite prepared to move so soon but there was no better time he could think of. He walked into Kenneth's without knocking. He never found a need to knock on the door of a place he owned. "Good news. We're moving."

Kenneth turned his head slowly. "Why? And how is that good news?"

"Allison's pregnant. And I bought us a whole bunch of land."

"I like it here. I don't want to leave."

Maxwell rolled his eyes and sighed. "You don't really have a choice since I own your house. It's going up for sale tomorrow. I'd start packing." It wasn't going to take him long. Maxwell provided Kenneth with what he needed to live comfortably but nothing more. He made a weekly food shopping trip and always brought Kenneth enough for the week. He had purchased a few articles of clothing and paid all his bills. When he bought the house, he furnished it with a gently used sofa, table, and chair and he moved the bed Kenneth had from their grandparent's.

Kenneth's brow furrowed and his bottom lip stuck out like it used to when he was little. "Can I convince you to let me stay here? There isn't really any reason I should have to leave, is there?"

"You're not staying. I already bought you a house. And I'm building two more."

"Two? Why two?"

"Don't worry about that. The point is, you're moving. You don't really want to be hours away from each other, do you?"

Kenneth didn't respond directly to the question. "I'll start packing."

Maxwell stopped and picked up dinner on his way home. He hoped Allison would be as happy about the move as he was. In the two years they had been together, she had never requested to leave or go anywhere. As far as he knew, she stayed at the cabin all day and only went out when he was with her. Most days she would make him dinner and lunch if he was home. He set the expectation early on that their home should be clean and she willingly made sure it was.

He had grown to love the isolation the cabin provided and he hoped the new location would afford the same comfort. He was happy he had at least one house built on the land and it was ready to go. He had purchased Kenneth's new house because it was close to where his land was but still far enough away that no one would be able to walk to it. He had no desire to put Kenneth and Allison within a distance where they would be able to see each other in his absence.

He wasn't sure what to expect when he broke the news to Allison but it didn't matter. Her reaction was exactly what he wanted. She took less than a minute to process the information and responded with a simple, "okay." The next day he brought home some moving boxes and Allison began immediately filling them up. He couldn't have asked for anything more.

Maxwell stopped in the middle of the road. "Well, these are the two houses I was telling you about. Which would you prefer?"

"Allison got out of the car and squinted her eyes. The houses were very far apart and she couldn't see much about either of them. She took a minute to look back and forth between them and got back in the car. "I think I'd like that one. I feel like it'll have a better view in the fall. Plus, the other one seems like it's missing something."

"Good choice. And you're right. The other house isn't finished yet." The road was no more than a few tire tracks in an overgrown field. The ground was rutted and the bottom of the car slammed down every time the tires hit one. "I know it doesn't look like much now but the land is beautiful. Once we mow down the overgrowth, you'll be able to see it. There's a lawnmower on the side of the house you can use. I brought it up last week."

Allison's mouth opened but nothing came out at first. She waited until they pulled up to the house to say anything. "Have you seen how big this field is? And you know I've never used a lawnmower before, right? I grew up in the city."

"Well, then it's about time you learned. I'll show you how it works in the morning."

She didn't know what to say. A part of her thought he might be joking but his tone of voice told her her wasn't. She just hoped he knew she wouldn't be able to do this in a few month's time. She got out of the car and started to walk around the back of the house, curious what she might find.

Maxwell cleared his throat. "It's dinner time and the kitchen's inside." He pointed toward the front door.

Allison nodded her head. "I'll have plenty of time to explore."

He followed her inside. "There's not much to see. There's land, a little more land, some woods, and that's about it. But, once you clean up the yard, maybe you can plant some flowers or something."

Allison stopped walking and turned to face him. Her eyes were wet with tears. "Why are you being so mean? I'm just excited to be in a new place. I don't mind cleaning up, I just wanted to see what else might be around."

He reached out and ran his hand down her face. "I'm not being mean. I was simply telling you that you may have to spruce it up yourself. It's green. Nothing but green for miles around.

You may have fun planting some flowers. It'll add some color and maybe it can be a new hobby for you." He leaned forward and kissed her forehead. "In the meantime, you can make me some dinner."

Allison went to the kitchen while Maxwell went back to the car to collect their bags. Opening the refrigerator, she wondered if she really had a choice in which house she wanted since this one was already full of food.

Chapter IX

"*Did Allison ever question where you got all the money for food or land? Did she ever ask what you did for a living?*" Having already heard the key points of the story from Kenneth, the detective was still having trouble comprehending how Maxwell could have been so convincing that he did this sort of thing not once or twice, but over ten times.

Maxwell shook his head. "*She never questioned anything...until I brought Rebecca home.*"

"*Oh? What do you think changed at that point?*"

"*Well, probably because I was honest with her. That was the only time I told them straight out. I learned quick after that.*"

"*Can you elaborate on that?*'

"*When I brought Rebecca home, I took her to Allison's house the next day and introduced them* to each other. Neither of them were happy to hear that I had another wife. I thought they would be thrilled to have someone else to talk to, a friend in the neighborhood. They weren't."

The detective rolled his eyes. "Can you blame them? I don't think I would be happy to find out my wife had another husband."

"I don't see the problem. They had everything they needed: Clothes, food, shelter."

"A husband who beat them..."

"I corrected them."

The detective couldn't believe he was having this conversation with a grown man. Abuse was abuse, regardless of how fancy one tried to make it seem. "What's the difference?"

"I corrected them to let them know they did something wrong. There was a reason for it. My mother beat me and my brother. We didn't have to do anything. She would pull us out of bed and hit us just because she was angry with my father. We didn't deserve that."

"And you think your wives did? You couldn't have just had a conversation and told them they were wrong?"

"You know they don't listen that way. They don't learn."

"Mhm. And the children? Did you correct them, too?"

The look on Maxwell's face went from one of mild amusement to one of anger. "I never hit any of my children." He spoke through gritted teeth and the detective knew he hit a nerve.

"Really? You never hit any of them? What about the small crosses in the graveyard? What happened to those children?" He had to fight back the waves of nausea that were threatening to take over. This was the part of the questioning process he didn't want to have any part of. He had interviewed dozens of murderers throughout his career but it was different when it involved children. No matter how tenured or emotionally closed off a detective was, not one of them wanted anything to do with cases that involved children.

"I had no way of knowing if those children were mine. The last thing I was going to do was be caught in the same position my father was. I owned that property, I owned those women, and I owned those children. There was no way I was going to raise a child that wasn't my own."

"Have you ever heard of a paternity test?"

"What? And have record those children existed? No, thank you."

"What happened when you brought Rebecca home?"

Maxwell stood between his two wives, unsure of what to do or whose side to be on. He didn't know what to expect when he introduced them. He thought, at most, they might be a little upset with him but would get over it quickly. He never would have guessed they were going to lash out at each other and both turn to him for backup. They were all standing in the middle of Allison's living room and it seemed to grew smaller by the minute.

"You need to get out of my house. Right now." Allison never raised her voice about anything and at that moment, Maxwell was thankful they didn't have neighbors.

Rebecca turned to leave, not because she wanted to give in but because it was respectful since it was someone else's house. When she walked out the door she heard Allison's voice behind her.

"You, too. Get out!"

Maxwell stuck his head out the door and told Rebecca to go home without him. He closed the door quietly and slowly made his way back to where Allison was standing. The stared at each other for a moment, both more angry than they had been in years.

"I want you out." Allison spoke through clenched teeth and her voice was deep.

Without hesitation, Maxwell lunged forward and pinned Allison against the wall by her neck. His face was within inches of hers. "I don't know who you think you're talking to right now. If it wasn't for me, you would still be living on the streets wearing rags, with dirt on your face, and holes in your shoes. You may even have died by now if it wasn't for me. I'm responsible for everything you have and you will remember that and treat me with the respect I deserve."

Allison used what strength she had. She lifter her arms and forcefully pushed against his shoulders to make him move away from her.

Maxwell barely teetered. He raised his arm backhanded her face.

She winced and tears filled her eyes. She looked at him with her bottom jaw limp.

"As I said, you will treat me with respect. You have nothing and are nothing without me."

For six months, Allison and Rebecca never spoke. Allison was struggling with the fact that Maxwell only showed up every other night. For two months, she made him dinner that he didn't come home to eat. She began adjusting to his schedule and ate small meals like cereal or a sandwich when she didn't expect him to be there. She learned the hard way that she was expected to make dinner regardless of whether she thought he would be there or not.

She didn't know how to explain to him how difficult that was for her. She didn't mind making him dinner. She enjoyed cooking. The problem she had with it was making food that would never get eaten. Most days, she would eat her portion at night and then have leftovers for lunch the next day but she didn't eat as much as he did. She ended up throwing out half of the food. She knew he could afford it but as someone who scrounged through trashcans and dumpsters for years, hoping to find something edible without flies or mold on, it sent her into a emotional state that she wasn't able to articulate. She wanted to make him happy, she wanted to be a good wife. But it was hard for her knowing what some had to go through to get a decent meal. She tried to speak to Maxwell about it and he laughed it off and told her she needed to get over it.

Rebecca stayed cooped up inside her house. She never even went out to the front porch. She wanted to go outside and enjoy the sunshine. She wanted to take a walk and see more of the land. There were pink, purple, and yellow wildflowers that she could see from her kitchen window and she wanted to see them close up. But she didn't want to risk running into Allison if she decided to do the same thing.

In Rebecca's mind, it was Allison's fault for not keeping her husband happy. If she would have just given him what he needed, he wouldn't have needed to stray. And she wouldn't be in this position. She was tired of having to share her husband with someone else. She loved him and she wanted him to give all his love to her. She knew she owed him something for keeping her fed, clothed, and sheltered, but she didn't believe having him sleeping with another women was a way to cover her debt to him.

She was allowing it to eat away at her and was becoming more depressed by the day. She never wanted to make him mad but she had enough. Over dinner one night, she asked him to get rid of Allison. She didn't care where she went or what he did with her, but she wanted her gone. She thought he would appreciate her desire to have him to herself. He didn't. He responded by giving her a black eye and bruised jaw. It was a week before she was able to eat without pain.

She took that time to consider what she was doing. It was clear Maxwell wouldn't be getting rid of Allison. If it really was going to be just the three of them, she thought maybe she needed to try to befriend her. She was lonely and she had no doubt Allison had to feel the same. She made a plan to go apologize the next day. For the meantime, she thought it might be best if she at least went outside. It was a small step but one she wasn't willing to make even a few weeks ago.

From her front porch, she could see a third house in the distance. She was sure it hadn't been there before. Curiosity got the best of her and before she knew it, she was past the end of her driveway and half-way to the new structure. From here, she saw a woman walk from the house to the car and back to the house. She thought it was her mind playing tricks on her but she wanted to be sure.

The next day, as she promised herself she would, she put on some makeup to cover the purple and yellow bruises and made her way to Allison's. She walked all the way to the door, raised her hand to knock, and froze. She turned and walked back down the steps and then reversed again. One of them had to make the first move.

Allison answered the door with watery, red eyes. "Rebecca?"

She didn't know why she was so surprised. She was the only other person here.

Allison opened her door wide and stepped aside, allowing Rebecca to enter. "I'm sorry for my appearance. I'm a little upset this morning." She gasped and grabbed Rebecca's arm, startling her. "Honey. Your face." She didn't try to hide anything. If it happened to her, she should have known he was doing it to Rebecca as well. "Don't be embarrassed. I had one almost identical last week."

At those words, Rebecca started to cry. The emotions took over before she could stop them. "I wanted to come over to apologize to you. I know this whole thing is not your fault. It...well, it was just easier to blame you than it was to blame him. I wanted so bad to be his one and only. And I didn't know what to do when I found out."

Allison reached her arms out and pulled Rebecca to her, hugging her tight. "I understand. I wanted the same thing. And I had it for a while. It was wonderful. But I also wanted to blame you because I felt like you stole my husband from me.

"I went outside yesterday. It was my first time going out at all since I got here. I saw another house." She closed her eyes and let her head drop. "And another woman."

Allison nodded. "That's what I'm upset about today. He told me last night he was bringing someone else to live here. I begged him not to but he said it was too late. He didn't tell you?"

Rebecca shook her head. "No. He didn't say anything."

"Okay. Let's have some coffee and I'll fill you in on what he told me."

Allison set out some cookies while the coffee brewed and then joined Rebecca at the table. "There's not really a lot to say. Maxwell just told me last night and I instinctively had the same reaction I did with you. But this time, after I thought about it for a few minutes, I wasn't angry anymore. I was hurt. I tried to ask him why but he wouldn't give me an answer. What he told me was that we are not, under any circumstances, allowed to tell this new woman that we're his wives." She choked out the last sentence. She had never said that out loud before and it was harder than she thought it would be. "He said he would tell her when he was ready."

Rebecca cocked her head and squinted her eyes. "What are we supposed to do if she asks? We can't avoid her forever. And if we don't go over to welcome her to the neighborhood, she's bound to come introduce herself at some point."

Allison nodded as she spoke. "I know. I tried to tell Maxwell that but he didn't want to hear it. He put his foot down and we need to listen. I don't want to find out what will happen if we don't."

They spent the next two hours chatting about anything they could think of. They were both surprised to find they had a lot in common. Allison was glad Rebecca took the time to visit. She felt a lot better after spending the afternoon with her and she knew they would become friends after all.

Rebecca was right. Janie made it three days before she went to visit the other two women. She stopped by Rebecca's first. They had a fun, lengthy conversation. She was so busy talking about everything she could think of, Janie didn't ask any questions about their situation. She did ask a lot of general questions but Rebecca could scarcely get a word in to answer any of them.

Allison had the same experience the first time they met.

On her sixth day there, Janie made her way to Rebecca's again and found Allison sitting at her kitchen table. She smiled. "The whole crew is here." Her face dropped as the statement came out of her mouth. She remained standing but looked back and forth between Allison and Rebecca. The first two women glanced at each other as they both began to panic. Janie slid into an empty chair and stared straight ahead, trying to process what she was thinking.

No one spoke. It was an awkward silence but no one wanted to be the one to break it.

Janie finally sighed and cleared her throat. "How do you two know Maxwell?"

Rebecca began to breathe heavily and Allison tapped her knee under the table to assure her it was okay. "He owns our homes." She said in in a matter of fact way, hoping it didn't leave any room for additional questions.

"Mhm. Neither of you have a car?"

"No." They responded in unison.

"Do you work?"

"Neither of us do."

Janie grunted. "How do you get food? How do you pay your bills?" She knew she sounded like she was accusing them of something and she didn't care, but she she wasn't sure what she was accusing them of. She was confused.

Rebecca answered her. "I think, maybe you need to talk to Maxwell if you have questions. He can explain it better than either of us would be able to."

Janie glared at her. "You think my husband knows more about your financial situation than you do?"

"I just think that instead of interrogating people you just met, maybe you should talk to your husband first."

"Fine." Janie got up and stormed out of the house, slamming the door behind her.

Chapter X

Maxwell stood and stretched again. "Can we please take a break? I've had to use the bathroom for about two hours. I'm tired, I'm hungry. Why do you need all this information if you already know about all of it?"

"It's standard procedure. When you go to court, we're going to have to tell the judge whether you were honest or not. If you are, the sentencing can land in your favor. We're almost done. Just a few more questions."

"Fine. Let's get them over with."

"When you brought Rebecca home, is that when the abuse started?"

Maxwell nodded. "I had never hit Allison until that night. Something inside me just snapped. I gave her everything and she told me to get out of my own house."

"And Rebecca?"

"After that first night with Allison, I couldn't stop."

"Did you ever think about your mother while you were hurting your wives? Did you remember how it made you feel when your mother hit you?"

He nodded again. "I thought of my mother every time. That's where the anger came from. I'm not going to try to deny that, detective. But these women could stand up for themselves. They weren't innocent children."

"You never hit any of your children?"

"Never. And you already asked me that."

"Can you tell me about the graveyard? Do you feel bad, at all, about the number of people you murdered?"

"Not really. It sucks that they didn't turn out to love me as much as I thought. We have a good thing going. Everyone who loves there is happy. Ask them, they'll tell you."

"We did ask them. And they weren't happy. They were grateful for the loving family but the common theme among all your wives was that they didn't love you."

"Bullshit." Maxwell stood and threw his chair against the two-way mirror. "Every single one of those women love me. They proved it to me every day."

He made a note in his notebook. "Okay, we'll go with that. What happened recently that caused all of this? Why did your brother end up calling us in a panic?"

"Because my brother betrayed me."

"Your brother did what he should have done years ago. He saved himself and the lives of everyone living on your property." He stared at Maxwell, daring him to argue. "So, what happened? What led to this final battle?"

It was weeks before either woman saw Janie again. They had no idea if she had asked Maxwell the truth or if she was choosing to stay away because she felt they were being dishonest with her. When she did finally arrive at Allison's door, she hung her head with shame. "I'm sorry I was mean to you guys. I didn't know."

Allison smiled but it was filled with sadness. "It's okay. We understand. But please know, we weren't allowed to say anything."

"I understand. Maxwell told me everything."

Over the next four years, three more women arrived: Samantha, Courtney, and Megan. They all went through similar periods of shame, hate, and depression. After isolating themselves for a few weeks, or a few months in Courtney's case, they made their way back out and did their best to act friendly with the others. They all got along and acted like any neighbor would. It was only when Maxwell was brought up they all showed signs of discomfort.

During lunch one afternoon, Courtney confided in Samantha and Allison that she was leaving. She had gone out numerous times during the night to see if she could find a way that would most likely bring her to civilization the fastest. Once she confirmed which route she was going to take, she invited the women to go with her. Neither Samantha nor Allison wanted anything to do with her plan. Samantha was pregnant and

Allison had two children she needed to worry about. Neither was willing to risk it.

That night, Allison walked to the main road to meet Maxwell when he got home. Maxwell brought his vehicle to a stop and Allison climbed in. He stared at her. "This is different. What do you want?"

Allison sighed. "I'm not really sure of the best way to let you know so I'm just going to say it. Courtney is planning on leaving...tonight. She said she found a path that she thinks will allow her to find other people and the police. She asked Samantha and I to go with her." She stopped talking and waited for him to process what she had told him.

"What did you tell her?"

"We told her 'no'. Neither of us is going anywhere. We tried to talk her out of it but her mind is made up."

Maxwell nodded. "Did she tell you which way she was going?"

"She did."

Maxwell spent the entire next week at Allison's house. They had heart felt conversations every night and he confided in her about stuff he had never told anyone else. He told her about his brother. He made up lies about why he didn't get any of their inheritance. He wasn't willing to tell her everything but the pieces he did choose to tell made him feel a lot better. After she told him about Courtney, Maxwell began to feel he could trust her completely. He tested it by bringing her with him when he went to get food for everyone. Allison reverted back to the first couple of days they were together and didn't speak to anyone while they were out.

No one had heard from Courtney and they were beginning to get suspicious. Megan was the only one brave enough to ask Maxwell about it. She went to Allison's house and asked to speak to him. The three of them sat in the living room. "You have to know that all of us talk to each other and none of us have heard anything from Courtney in the last. That's weird. We'd like to know if she's okay."

Maxwell grunted. "I'm well aware of how you all are. This is what you can tell everyone: Courtney is gone. All mentions of her stops immediately when you have the conversation with the others. Her name is not to be brought up again. And it would be in all of your best interests to not try to pull the same stunt she did." He got up and walked out the back door.

"Should we bring everyone together tomorrow?"

Allison nodded. "Maxwell is going out of town in the morning. Ask them all to meet here."

Megan agreed and left.

The next afternoon, all the women met at Allison's house and were given the same information Megan and Allison had been.

"How did Maxwell find out she was planning on leaving? Did she tell him?"

Allison took a deep breath. "I told him." She could feel the cold stares coming from four different directions.

"Why would you do that?"

"Because he needed to know. Do you have any idea what he would have done to all of us if he found out we knew and didn't say anything?"

"We don't even know where she went. He could have killed her for all we know. If he did, that's your fault. How could you do that?"

"He could have killed one or all of us if we didn't tell him. I did what I thought I had to do to protect the rest of us. We told her not to go and she wouldn't listen. We tried."

Janie stood and walked out the door, followed by the rest of the women. It was months before anyone spoke to Allison again.

Fifteen

Years

Later

Allison and Maxwell hadn't been getting along. Allison was lonely and felt isolated by everyone. None of the women, except Kathleen, were speaking to her. She began questioning everything Maxwell did and threatened to leave on multiple occasions. He dared her to, knowing she would never have the courage to try.

One afternoon, she saw Kenneth's car parked in the driveway of one of the newest wives. Her name was Joanna and she had been feeling ill for over a week. Allison was relieved to see Maxwell had finally called the doctor. She was equally happy that she would get to talk to him. She had been waiting for months. She didn't know how long she would have to wait but she didn't care. She put on her jacket and made her way toward the main road. When she felt she was far enough away from the houses, she hid behind a large boulder and waited until she could see his car coming toward the road.

When he approached, she jumped out in front of him causing him to have to slam on the brakes. Once the car came to a stop, she ran to the driver's side and ripped the door open. "You're going to stay here and you're going to talk to me." She didn't leave him any room to argue.

She slipped into the back seat, the only way she could think of so he didn't have a chance to drive off. "Kenneth, this has gone on long enough."

"How do you know my first name?" He had craned his neck to be able to see her face. He was told never to tell any of the women or the children what his first name was.

"Because Maxwell told me. He's told me a lot."

"I don't believe you. Maxwell would never tell anyone who I am." His face had turned crimson and he was sweating. His heart raced in his chest.

Allison laughed. She couldn't believe Maxwell was doing it to him, too. "You don't believe me? What if I told you I know you didn't get any of the inheritance from your parents or your grandparents? What if I told you I know you're his brother. What if I told you I know you never went to medical school, or college at all for that matter, and didn't even finish high school? What if I told you I know he was driving when you two got in that accident and I know he killed your parents? Would you believe me then?"

Kenneth's eyes were wet and he was forcing himself not to break down in tears. "How do you know that?" He had to fight to get the words to come out.

"Why haven't you helped us? You have a car. You can go find help any time you want. Why are you allowing him to hurt us? Why are you allowing him to control you?"

"Because Maxwell has connections. He gets everything he wants. If I try to go find help, he'll find out and he'll kill me."

"You really think he has connections all the way out here?"

"He told me he does."

Allison laughed until tears formed in her eyes. "Wow. You know he's a liar, right? He's lied to all of time and time again. He's lied to you. He forces you to lie to all of us. What on Earth would make you think he's telling the truth about this?"

"I can't help. I'm have nothing without him. He's taken everything."

She nodded. "I know. He's done the same to everyone here. So, I have a plan. This is what you're going to do..."

The next time Allison saw Maxwell she told him she spoke to the doctor and got confirmation on everything Maxwell had confessed to her. "I really think you need to go speak to him because I he's ready to tell someone. He came over here after he left Joanna's the other day." She tried to sound as concerned as she could. "I know I haven't been fair to you lately and I'm sorry I threatened to leave. I hope you know I would never do it. I love you, Maxwell. And I appreciate everything you've done for me more than you'll ever know. I don't want the doctor to ruin that. I don't want him to destroy everything you've created. You really need to speak to him before he does something to rip us all apart."

Maxwell's only response was to agree that he would speak to him.

When he left the next morning, Allison dressed and ran out the door to Kathleen's house. She knew after he spoke to his brother, he would be coming back for her. She didn't know how much she trusted Kenneth but she kept her fingers crossed that he would hold up his end of the bargain. She knew Maxwell would most likely kill her but she had finally realized it would be worth it if it meant the other women could get away. She only hoped one of them would be kind enough to take in her children until they became adults.

By the time she reached Kathleen's house, she had worked herself up into a full panic. When she entered the house, she told Kathleen everything she knew and made her promise to tell anyone who would listen. She made her promise she would try to get away.

Her mind was in a spiral: hoping her plan worked, praying she didn't die, making peace with the reality that she might, keeping her fingers crossed that Kathleen would be able to figure out how to get out of this situation. She made her way back home and waited, anxiety eating away at her for hours.

When Maxwell arrived at Kenneth's house, he let himself in and stared at his brother. "Heard you talked to Allison." His voice was stern but not angry.

"Max. I didn't talk to her. She ran out to my car when I was leaving Joanna's. She made me listen to her but I didn't tell her anything. I swear."

"Why should I believe you?"

"Because it's the truth. I never said anything to her. She tried to tell me that she knew all this stuff about our family but she was wrong about most of it."

"What did she tell you?"

"Weird stuff. Some of it could be true but most of it wasn't. She said I'm older than you. She thinks grandma and grandpa took me out of their will because I had a head injury. I don't know how she knows I'm your brother. Did you tell her?"

"I did. But I'm not here to talk about that. Are you planning on telling someone what I've done?"

"No...no. I would never. I've helped you, for years. I'd be in just as much trouble as you. And I don't want you to leave, Max. You're all I have. Not only would you go away but I'd have nothing left." Panic sounded in his voice. "I would never do that to you, Max."

"What else did she tell you?"

Kenneth lowered his head and his voice softened even more than it was. "She told me she was going to tell Kathleen everything she knows. She didn't want to carry the burden of being the only one who knew the truth."

Maxwell nodded. "You're a good brother, Kenneth."

He didn't know how soon she would speak to Kathleen. He spent the next two days at Janie's house before he decided Allison would have had plenty of time to tell her.

Kenneth had his car parked behind the same boulder Allison had hid behind just a few days before. He watched Maxwell leave Janie's house and make his way to Kathleen's. He parked his car down the road a little way from her house and ran, crouched, to the window so he could see what was happening inside. He arrived just in time to see Kathleen grab the knife from the counter. He ran back to his car and sped all the way home before dialing the local police department.

Maxwell left Kathleen's house, still carrying the knife in his hand, and ran all the way to Allison's. He slammed the door open to find her sitting, waiting for him, on the couch.

Chapter XI

The detective was getting tired. He had taken two breaks in the last twelve hours and they were only to use the bathroom and refill his coffee. It was seven in the morning and he had been up for over twenty-four hours. "After everything that's happened, your childhood, all the women, the children...Allison seems to be the only person you care about. What was it about her that made her so special to you?"

Maxwell yawned, more from boredom than exhaustion. "After all the time you and I have spent together, you still don't understand?"

"No. Not really. You had over ten wives and you didn't seem to care about any of them. Except her."

He rolled his eyes toward the ceiling. "Allison was the only constant in my life. She loved me for *who I was. She never asked for anything. She was grateful for everything she had. Not one other woman ever even thanked me for bringing them out to dinner."*

"I can understand not feeling appreciated. You showed them interest, you paid for their meal, no doubt provided great conversation and companionship. And they didn't even thank you? That would upset anyone, I think." He stared at Maxwell waiting for any sort of response. He didn't get one. "I have to ask, if Allison was the one person who so willing to give you everything you needed...why bring the other women in at all? Why didn't you just keep the family with the two of you and your child?"

"Because, during her pregnancy, she stopped paying attention to me. She slept all the time, she wouldn't let me touch her. I wasn't getting my needs met, so I found it elsewhere."

"Okay, so you needed physical intimacy. That's not uncommon. But why bring the other women home? Why not just have an affair, get what you want without the commitment?"

"It's quite simple, really. I needed the intimacy at home, too. Physical and emotional. And, I didn't want to share them with anyone else. If they were going to be with me, they were going to be mine."

"You didn't want to share them with any one else but you made them all share you?"

"I didn't make them do anything they didn't want to."

The detective flipped back through his notebook, not because he needed to, he simply wanted to add some dramatic flair. "I'm just checking my notes here to make sure we're on the same page." He stopped flipping the papers and looked hard at Maxwell. "You beat these women into submission. You lied to them, manipulated them, told them they were never allowed to leave. You cut all ties they had with friends and family and moved them to the middle of nowhere so they had no contact with the outside world."

"They came with me willingly. And none of them ever left."

"Because you murdered the few that tried." He was doing his best to keep his composure but the last statement came out much louder than he intended and he found himself leaning over the metal table, inches from Maxwell's face.

Maxwell smiled viciously. He leaned back and crossed his arms over his chest. "But they never left."

The detective stood and tossed his chair into the corner of the room before storming out. He needed a break. He had to get some fresh air and take a few deep breaths. When he reentered the room, he casually picked his chair up and reclaimed his seat across from Maxwell and smiled. "Do you still feel the same way about Allison now as you did when you married her?"

"Always. Allison was my one true love. I didn't want to hurt her. I didn't want to kill her. But she

betrayed me just like everyone else did. I did what I had to do to protect what I had made. And everything would have been fine if it wasn't for Kenneth."

One

Year

Later

Maxwell heard the familiar buzz of a secured door being opened. His shoulders tensed at the thought of his brother walking through the door. After everything they had been through, Kenneth sold him out, traded his knowledge for probation while Maxwell would spend his remaining years in prison.

Leaning forward, over the table, his eyes shifted to the door when he heard the familiar clacking of heels against the cement floor. A key turned in the lock and the door opened slowly. His eyes widened and he gasped. "Allison?"

She smiled wide and the guard closed the door behind her. "Maxwell." Her confidence showed in her posture and in the sound of her voice.

Maxwell stammered. "You...you shouldn't be here."

She nodded. "That's what I came to talk to you about." She moved to the center of the room and locked her eyes on his.

For the first time since they met, Maxwell could feel her presence looming over him. He felt like a child again, trapped in his mother's gaze. His head felt foggy and his body began to shake against his will.

"You were so smart, for so many years. You made one woman after the next fall in love with you. You convinced them to trust you. You covered your tracks. And the one time you needed to be careful, you let your guard down."

She frowned and shook her head. She was disappointed in him. "See, you should have checked to make sure I was dead. I was the one person who knew all your secrets, the only legal wife you had. You didn't plan far enough ahead when you married me. Legally, everything you owned was...is...half mine. Those papers you had me sign...they only stop me from accessing your money if we get divorced and I have no intention of doing that. So..." She took a slow lap around the room and Maxwell followed her with his eyes. He didn't seem to be able to move any other part of his body.

"Since you no longer have a need for money or any other physical possessions, I took it upon myself to distribute all of it. I sold the property we were living on as well as that beat up cabin across from where your parents died. I got rid of your truck and emptied every one of your bank accounts. All of them. After all was said and done, each of your remaining wives and your brother was gifted just over four million dollars. So, in case you were concerned about how we would all survive in your absence...don't worry. We'll all be just fine."

Allison turned on her heel and banged her fist against the metal door. When it opened, she slipped through without looking back.

Author's Note

When you are finished reading, if you do not keep physical books, please consider donating your copy to your local library for their book sale or to your local prison book program.

Author's Bio

Trish recently moved across the country where she found her forever home, enjoying the desert sunshine and wildlife all year long. She was born and raised in a small town in northern Connecticut. Growing up, she was always fascinated by unsolved mysteries and true crimes as well as the psychological elements behind them. As an avid reader, her go to books are thrillers, suspense, and true crime. *Nursery's Rhyme* is Trish's first novel.

Made in United States
North Haven, CT
22 October 2022

25778613R00088